BOOKS BY MARK STRAND

POETRY

The Continuous Life 1990
Selected Poems 1980
The Late Hour 1978
The Story of Our Lives 1973
Darker 1970
Reasons for Moving 1968
Sleeping with One Eye Open 1964

PROSE

Mr. and Mrs. Baby 1985
The Monument 1978

TRANSLATIONS

Travelling in the Family 1986
(POEMS BY CARLOS DRUMMOND DE ANDRADE,
WITH THOMAS COLCHIE)
The Owl's Insomnia 1973
(POEMS BY RAFAEL ALBERTI)

ART BOOKS

William Bailey 1987
Art of the Real 1983

FOR CHILDREN

The Planet of Lost Things 1982
The Night Book 1985
Rembrandt Takes a Walk 1986

ANTHOLOGIES

Another Republic (WITH CHARLES SIMIC) 1976
New Poetry of Mexico (WITH OCTAVIO PAZ) 1970
The Contemporary American Poets 1969

REASONS FOR MOVING

DARKER

& THE SARGENTVILLE NOTEBOOK

MARK STRAND

for Gary

with thanks and best wishes

P O E M S

REASONS FOR MOVING

DARKER

& THE SARGENTVILLE NOTEBOOK

Mark Strand

ALFRED A. KNOPF, NEW YORK, 1992

THIS IS A BORZOI BOOK
PUBLISHED BY ALFRED A. KNOPF, INC.

These three titles were originally published separately:
Reasons for Moving and *Darker*, Atheneum;
and *The Sargentville Notebook*, Burning Deck.

Library of Congress Cataloging-in-Publication Data
Strand, Mark, [date]
    [Poems]
    Reasons for moving ; Darker ; and The Sargentville notebook :
poems / by Mark Strand. — 1st ed.
    p.   cm.
    ISBN 0-679-73668-9 (pbk.)
    I. Title: Reasons for moving. II. Title: Darker. III. Title:
Sargentville notebook.
PS3569.T69A6 1992
811'.54—dc20   91-53125
                                                   CIP

Manufactured in the United States of America
First Edition

CONTENTS

REASONS FOR MOVING

DARKER

I   *Giving Myself Up*

II *Black Maps*

III *My Life By Somebody Else*

REASONS FOR MOVING

EATING POETRY

Ink runs from the corners of my mouth.
There is no happiness like mine.
I have been eating poetry.

The librarian does not believe what she sees.
Her eyes are sad
and she walks with her hands in her dress.

The poems are gone.
The light is dim.
The dogs are on the basement stairs and coming up.

Their eyeballs roll,
their blond legs burn like brush.
The poor librarian begins to stamp her feet and weep.

She does not understand.
When I get on my knees and lick her hand,
she screams.

I am a new man.
I snarl at her and bark.
I romp with joy in the bookish dark.

THE ACCIDENT

A train runs over me.
I feel sorry
for the engineer
who crouches down
and whispers in my ear
that he is innocent.

He wipes my forehead,
blows the ashes
from my lips.
My blood steams
in the evening air,
clouding his glasses.

He whispers in my ear
the details of his life—
he has a wife
and child he loves,
he's always been
an engineer.

He talks
until the beam
from someone's flashlight
turns us white.
He stands.
He shakes his jacket out

and starts to run.
The cinders crack
under his boots,
the air is cold
and thick
against his cheeks.

Back home he sits
in the kitchen,
staring at the dark.
His face is flushed,
his hands are pressed
between his knees.

He sees me sprawled
and motionless
beside the tracks
and the faint blooms
of my breath
being swept away;

the fields bend
under the heavy sheets
of the wind
and birds scatter
into the rafters
of the trees.

He rushes
from the house,
lifts the wreckage
of my body in his arms
and brings me back.
I lie in bed.

He puts his head
down next to mine
and tells me
that I'll be all right.
A pale light
shines in his eyes.

I listen to the wind
press hard against the house.
I cannot sleep.
I cannot stay awake.
The shutters bang.
The end of my life begins.

THE MAILMAN

It is midnight.
He comes up the walk
and knocks at the door.
I rush to greet him.
He stands there weeping,
shaking a letter at me.
He tells me it contains
terrible personal news.
He falls to his knees.
"Forgive me! Forgive me!" he pleads.

I ask him inside.
He wipes his eyes.
His dark blue suit
is like an inkstain
on my crimson couch.
Helpless, nervous, small,
he curls up like a ball
and sleeps while I compose
more letters to myself
in the same vein:

"You shall live
by inflicting pain.
You shall forgive."

THE MAN IN THE TREE

I sat in the cold limbs of a tree.
I wore no clothes and the wind was blowing.
You stood below in a heavy coat,
the coat you are wearing.

And when you opened it, baring your chest,
white moths flew out, and whatever you said
at that moment fell quietly onto the ground,
the ground at your feet.

Snow floated down from the clouds into my ears.
The moths from your coat flew into the snow.
And the wind as it moved under my arms, under my chin,
whined like a child.

I shall never know why
our lives took a turn for the worse, nor will you.
Clouds sank into my arms and my arms rose.
They are rising now.

I sway in the white air of winter
and the starling's cry lies down on my skin.
A field of ferns covers my glasses; I wipe them away
in order to see you.

I turn and the tree turns with me.
Things are not only themselves in this light.
You close your eyes and your coat
falls from your shoulders,

the tree withdraws like a hand,
the wind fits into my breath, yet nothing is certain.
The poem that has stolen these words from my mouth
may not be this poem.

THE GHOST SHIP

Through the crowded street
It floats,

Its vague
Tonnage like wind.

It glides
Through the sadness

Of slums
To the outlying fields.

Slowly,
Now by an ox,

Now by a windmill,
It moves.

Passing
At night like a dream

Of death,
It cannot be heard;

Under the stars
It steals.

Its crew
And passengers stare;

Whiter than bone,
Their eyes

Do not
Turn or close.

THE KITE

for Bill and Sandy Bailey

It rises over the lake, the farms,
The edge of the woods,
And like a body without arms
Or legs it swings
Blind and blackening in the moonless air.
The wren, the vireo, the thrush
Make way. The rush
And flutter of wings
Fall through the dark
Like a mild rain.
We cover our heads and ponder
The farms and woods that rim
The central lake.
A barred owl sits on a limb
Silent as bark.
An almost invisible
Curtain of rain seems to come nearer.
The muffled crack and drum
Of distant thunder
Blunders against our ears.

A row of hills appears.
It sinks into a valley
Where farms and woods surround a lake.
There is no rain.
It is impossible to say what form
The weather will take.
We blow on our hands,
Trying to keep them warm,
Hoping it will not snow.
Birds fly overhead.
A man runs by
Holding the kite string.
He does not see us standing dark
And still as mourners under the sullen sky.
The wind cries in his lapels. Leaves fall
As he moves by them.
His breath blooms in the chill
And for a time it seems that small
White roses fill the air,
Although we are not sure.

Inside the room
The curtains fall like rain.
Darkness covers the flower-papered walls,
The furniture and floors,
Like a mild stain.
The mirrors are emptied, the doors
Quietly closed. The man, asleep
In the heavy arms of a chair,
Does not see us
Out in the freezing air
Of the dream he is having.
The beating of wings and the wind
Move through the deep,
Echoing valley. The kite
Rises over the lake,
The farms, the edge of the woods
Into the moonless night
And disappears.
And the man turns in his chair,
Slowly beginning to wake.

THE MARRIAGE

The wind comes from opposite poles,
traveling slowly.

She turns in the deep air.
He walks in the clouds.

She readies herself,
shakes out her hair,

makes up her eyes,
smiles.

The sun warms her teeth,
the tip of her tongue moistens them.

He brushes the dust from his suit
and straightens his tie.

He smokes.
Soon they will meet.

The wind carries them closer.
They wave.

Closer, closer.
They embrace.

She is making a bed.
He is pulling off his pants.

They marry
and have a child.

The wind carries them off
in different directions.

The wind is strong, he thinks
as he straightens his tie.

I like this wind, she says
as she puts on her dress.

The wind unfolds.
The wind is everything to them.

THE WHOLE STORY

— I'd rather you didn't feel it necessary to tell him, "That's a fire. And what's more, we can't do anything about it, because we're on this train, see?"

How it should happen this way
I am not sure, but you
Are sitting next to me,
Minding your own business
When all of a sudden I see
A fire out the window.

I nudge you and say,
"That's a fire. And what's more,
We can't do anything about it,
Because we're on this train, see?"
You give me an odd look
As though I had said too much.

But for all you know I may
Have a passion for fires,
And travel by train to keep
From having to put them out.
It may be that trains
Can kindle a love of fire.

I might even suspect
That you are a fireman
In disguise. And then again
I might be wrong. Maybe
You are the one
Who loves a good fire. Who knows?

Perhaps you are elsewhere,
Deciding that with no place
To go you should not
Take a train. And I,
Seeing my own face in the window
May have lied about the fire.

THE BABIES

Let us save the babies.
Let us run downtown.
The babies are screaming.

You shall wear mink
and your hair shall be done.
I shall wear tails.

Let us save the babies
even if we run in rags
to the heart of town.

Let us not wait for tomorrow.
Let us drive into town
and save the babies.

Let us hurry.
They lie in a warehouse
with iron windows and iron doors.

The sunset pink of their skin
is beginning to glow.
Their teeth

poke through their gums
like tombstones.
Let us hurry.

They have fallen asleep.
Their dreams
are infecting them.

Let us hurry.
Their screams rise
from the warehouse chimney.

We must move faster.
The babies have grown into their suits.
They march all day in the sun without blinking.

Their leader sits in a bullet-proof car and applauds.
Smoke issues from his helmet.
We cannot see his face:

we are still running.
More babies than ever are locked in the warehouse.
Their screams are like sirens.

We are still running to the heart of town.
Our clothes are getting ragged.
We shall not wait for tomorrow.

The future is always beginning now.
The babies are growing into their suits.
Let us run to the heart of town.

Let us hurry.
Let us save the babies.
Let us try to save the babies.

THE LAST BUS

(Rio de Janeiro, 1966)

It is dark.
A slight rain
dampens the streets.
Nothing moves

in Lota's park.
The palms hang
over the matted grass,
and the voluminous bushes,

bundled in sheets,
billow beside the walks.
The world is out of reach.
The ghosts of bathers rise

slowly out of the surf and turn
high in the spray.
They walk on the beach
and their eyes burn

like stars.
And Rio sleeps:
the sea is a dream
in which it dies and is reborn.

The bus speeds.
A violet cloud
unravels in its wake.
My legs begin to shake.

My lungs fill up with steam.
Sweat covers my face
and falls to my chest.
My neck and shoulders ache.

Not even sure
that I am awake,
I grip the hot
edge of the seat.

The driver smiles.
His pants are rolled above his knees
and his bare calves
gleam in the heat.

A woman tries to comfort me.
She puts her hand under my shirt
and writes the names of flowers
on my back.

Her skirt is black.
She has a tiny skull
and crossbones on each knee.
There is a garden in her eyes

where rows of dull,
white tombstones crowd the air
and people stand,
waving goodbye.

I have the feeling I am there.
She whispers through her teeth
and puts her lips
against my cheek.

The driver turns.
His eyes are closed and he is combing
back his hair.
He tells me to be brave.

I feel my heartbeat
growing fainter as he speaks.
The woman kisses me again.
Her jaw creaks

and her breath clings
to my neck like mist.
I turn to the window's
cracked pane

streaked with rain.
Where have I been?
I look toward Rio—
nothing is the same.

The Christ who stood
in a pool of electric light
high on his hill
is out of sight.

And the bay is black.
And the black city
sinks into its grave.
And I shall never come back.

WHAT TO THINK OF

Think of the jungle,
The green steam rising.

It is yours.
You are the prince of Paraguay.

Your minions kneel
Deep in the shade of giant leaves

While you drive by
Benevolent as gold.

They kiss the air
That moments before

Swept over your skin,
And rise only after you've passed.

Think of yourself, almost a god,
Your hair on fire,

The bellows of your heart pumping.
Think of the bats

Rushing out of their caves
Like a dark wind to greet you;

Of the vast nocturnal cities
Of lightning bugs

Floating down
From Minas Gerais;

Of the coral snakes;
Of the crimson birds

With emerald beaks;
Of the tons and tons of morpho butterflies

Filling the air
Like the cold confetti of paradise.

THE DIRTY HAND

My hand is dirty.
I must cut it off.
To wash it is pointless.
The water is putrid.
The soap is bad.
It won't lather.
The hand is dirty.
It's been dirty for years.

I used to keep it
out of sight,
in my pants pocket.
No one suspected a thing.
People came up to me,
wanting to shake hands.
I would refuse
and the hidden hand,
like a dark slug,
would leave its imprint
on my thigh.
And then I realized
it was the same
if I used it or not.
Disgust was the same.

Ah! How many nights
in the depths of the house
I washed that hand,
scrubbed it, polished it,
dreamed it would turn
to diamond or crystal
or even, at last,
into a plain white hand,
the clean hand of a man,
that you could shake,
or kiss, or hold
in one of those moments
when two people confess
without saying a word . . .
Only to have
the incurable hand,
lethargic and crablike,
open its dirty fingers.

And the dirt was vile.
It was not mud or soot
or the caked filth
of an old scab
or the sweat
of a laborer's shirt.
It was a sad dirt
made of sickness
and human anguish.
It was not black;
black is pure.
It was dull,
a dull grayish dirt.

It is impossible
to live with this
gross hand that lies
on the table
Quick! Cut it off!
Chop it to pieces
and throw it
into the ocean.
With time, with hope
and its intricate workings
another hand will come,
pure, transparent as glass,
and fasten itself to my arm.

THE TUNNEL

A man has been standing
in front of my house
for days. I peek at him
from the living room
window and at night,
unable to sleep,
I shine my flashlight
down on the lawn.
He is always there.

After a while
I open the front door
just a crack and order
him out of my yard.
He narrows his eyes
and moans. I slam
the door and dash back
to the kitchen, then up
to the bedroom, then down.

I weep like a schoolgirl
and make obscene gestures
through the window. I
write large suicide notes
and place them so he
can read them easily.
I destroy the living
room furniture to prove
I own nothing of value.

When he seems unmoved
I decide to dig a tunnel
to a neighboring yard.
I seal the basement off
from the upstairs with
a brick wall. I dig hard
and in no time the tunnel
is done. Leaving my pick
and shovel below,

I come out in front of a house
and stand there too tired to
move or even speak, hoping
someone will help me.
I feel I'm being watched
and sometimes I hear
a man's voice,
but nothing is done
and I have been waiting for days.

MOONTAN

for Donald Justice

The bluish, pale
face of the house
rises above me
like a wall of ice

and the distant,
solitary
barking of an owl
floats toward me.

I half close my eyes,

Over the damp
dark of the garden
flowers swing
back and forth
like small balloons.

The solemn trees,
each buried
in a cloud of leaves,
seem lost in sleep.

It is late.
I lie in the grass,
smoking,
feeling at ease,
pretending the end
will be like this.

Moonlight
falls on my flesh.
A breeze
circles my wrist.

I drift.
I shiver.
I know that soon
the day will come
to wash away the moon's
white stain,

that I shall walk
in the morning sun
invisible
as anyone.

THE DREAM

The top of my head opens
and out you go
into the pink and violet light of morning.

How bold you are!
You rise like the moon
while I sit on the edge of my bed,

afraid to move.
A breeze comes in the window,
brushes against my cheek, and I feel you shiver.

You will not last the day
When they see you,
dogs will bark,

children will run to their mothers,
and birds will flock to you for shade.
You shrink at the thought.

Come back!
Bring the girls, the doctor, and the samba band!
There's plenty of room.

I shall close my eyes
and lie down in the dark
and look at you.

THE MAN IN BLACK

I was walking downtown
when I noticed a man in black,
black cape and black boots, coming toward me.

His arms out in front of him,
his fingers twinkling with little rings,
he looked like a summer night full of stars.

It was summer. The night was full of stars.
The tall buildings formed a hallway down which I walked.
The man in black came toward me.

The waxed tips of his mustache shone
like tiny spears and his teeth glistened.
I offered him my hand which he did not take.

I felt like a fool and stood in his black wake,
shaken and small, and my tears
swung back and forth in the sultry air like chandeliers.

VIOLENT STORM

Those who have chosen to pass the night
Entertaining friends
And intimate ideas in the bright,
Commodious rooms of dreams
Will not feel the slightest tremor
Or be wakened by what seems
Only a quirk in the dry run
Of conventional weather. For them,
The long night sweeping over these trees
And houses will have been no more than one
In a series whose end
Only the nervous or morbid consider.
But for us, the wide-awake, who tend
To believe the worst is always waiting
Around the next corner or hiding in the dry,
Unsteady branch of a sick tree, debating
Whether or not to fell the passerby,
It has a sinister air.
How we wish we were sunning ourselves
In a world of familiar views
And fixed conditions, confined
By what we know, and able to refuse
Entry to the unaccounted for. For now,
Deeper and darker than ever, the night unveils
Its dubious plans, and the rain
Beats down in gales
Against the roof. We sit behind
Closed windows, bolted doors,
Unsure and ill at ease

While the loose, untidy wind,
Making an almost human sound, pours
Through the open chambers of the trees.
We cannot take ourselves or what belongs
To us for granted. No longer the exclusive,
Last resorts in which we could unwind,
Lounging in easy chairs,
Recalling the various wrongs
We had been done or spared, our rooms
Seem suddenly mixed up in our affairs.
We do not feel protected
By the walls, nor can we hide
Before the duplicating presence
Of their mirrors, pretending we are the ones who stare
From the other side, collected
In the glassy air.
A cold we never knew invades our bones.
We shake as though the storm were going to hurl us down
Against the flat stones
Of our lives. All other nights
Seem pale compared to this, and the brilliant rise
Of morning after morning seems unthinkable.
Already now the lights
That shared our wakefulness are dimming
And the dark brushes against our eyes.

THE SUICIDE

I jump from a building
As if I were falling asleep,

The wind like a pillow
Slowing me down,

Slowing me down
As if I were dreaming.

Surrounded by air,
I come to a stop,

And stand like a tourist
Watching the pigeons.

People in offices,
Wanting to save me,

Open their mouths.
"Throw me a stone," I yell,

Wanting to fall.
But nobody listens.

They throw me a rope.
And now I am walking,

Talking to you,
Talking to you

As if I were dreaming
I were alive.

KEEPING THINGS WHOLE

In a field
I am the absence
of field.
This is
always the case.
Wherever I am
I am what is missing.

When I walk
I part the air
and always
the air moves in
to fill the spaces
where my body's been.

We all have reasons
for moving.
I move
to keep things whole.

THE DOOR

The door is before you again and the shrieking
Starts and the mad voice is saying here here.
The myth of comfort dies and the couch of her
Body turns to dust. Clouds enter your eyes.

It is autumn. People are jumping from jetliners;
Their relatives leap into the air to join them.
That is what the shrieking is about. Nobody wants
To leave, nobody wants to stay behind.

The door is before you and you are unable to speak.
Your breathing is slow and you peer through
The window. Your doctor is wearing a butcher's apron
And carries a knife. You approve.

And you remember the first time you came. The leaves
Spun from the maples as you ran to the house.
You ran as you always imagined you would.
Your hand is on the door. This is where you came in.

THE DEAD

The graves grow deeper.
The dead are more dead each night.

Under the elms and the rain of leaves,
The graves grow deeper.

The dark folds of the wind
Cover the ground. The night is cold.

The leaves are swept against the stones.
The dead are more dead each night.

A starless dark embraces them.
Their faces dim.

We cannot remember them
Clearly enough. We never will.

THE MAN IN THE MIRROR

for Decio de Souza

I walk down the narrow,
carpeted hall.
The house is set.
The carnation in my buttonhole

precedes me like a small
continuous explosion.
The mirror
is in the living room.

You are there.
Your face is white, unsmiling, swollen.
The fallen body of your hair
is dull and out of place.

Buried in the darkness of your pockets,
your hands are motionless.
You do not seem awake.
Your skin sleeps

and your eyes lie in the deep
blue of their sockets,
impossible to reach.
How long will all this take?

I remember how we used to stand
wishing the glass
would dissolve between us,
and how we watched our words

cloud that bland,
innocent surface,
and when our faces blurred
how scared we were.

But that was another life.
One day you turned away
and left me here
to founder in the stillness of your wake.

Your suit floating, your hair
moving like eel grass
in a shallow bay, you drifted
out of the mirror's room, through the hall

and into the open air.
You seemed to rise and fall
with the wind, the sway
taking you always farther away, farther away.

Darkness filled your sleeves.
The stars moved through you.
The vague music of your shrieking
blossomed in my ears.

I tried forgetting what I saw;
I got down on the floor,
pretending to be dead.
It did not work.

My heart bunched in my rib-cage like a bat,
blind and cowardly,
beating in and out,
a solemn, irreducible black.

The things you drove me to!
I walked in the calm of the house,
calling you back.
You did not answer.

I sat in a chair
and stared across the room.
The walls were bare.
The mirror was nothing without you.

I lay down on the couch
and closed my eyes.
My thoughts rose in the dark
like faint balloons,

and I would turn them over
one by one and watch them shiver.
I always fell into a deep
and arid sleep.

Then out of nowhere late one night
you reappeared,
a huge vegetable moon,
a bruise coated with light.

You stood before me,
dreamlike and obscene,
your face lost
under layers of heavy skin,

your body sunk in a green
and wrinkled sea of clothing.
I tried to help you
but you refused.

Days passed
and I would rest
my cheek against the glass,
wanting nothing but the old you.

I sang so sadly
that the neighbors wept
and dogs whined with pity.
Some things I wish I could forget.

You didn't care,
standing still while flies
collected in your hair
and dust fell like a screen before your eyes.

You never spoke
or, tried to come up close.
Why did I want so badly
to get through to you?

It still goes on.
I go into the living room and you are there.
You drift in a pool
of silver air

where wounds and dreams of wounds
rise from the deep
humus of sleep
to bloom like flowers against the glass.

I look at you
and see myself
under the surface.
A dark and private weather

settles down on everything.
It is colder
and the dreams wither away.
You stand

like a shade
in the painless glass,
frail, distant, older
than ever.

It will always be this way.
I stand here scared
that you will disappear,
scared that you will stay.

THE SARGENTVILLE NOTEBOOK

A man in Utah hates my work.
Do not disappoint him, Excellence.

She did her best to starve the air by growing fat.

When I am with you, I am two places at once.
When you are with me, you have just arrived
with a suitcase which you pack
with one hand and unpack with the other.

Is it something meaningful or not
that wakens the deep man
from his shallow sleep?

I am thinking of HB and RH and HM and SF
and WB and DJ as I sit reading HV on WS.

Wisdom in a dull man
is like prolonged applause.

He told himself she no longer existed.
When he saw her in the street
he knew he had seen her somewhere,
but could not place himself.

When a poet loves, he loves himself.
When he hates, he hates everybody else.

If I say it, it cannot be.
If I said it, I didn't.

The poet could not speak of himself,
but only of the gradations leading toward him and away.

What shall we do, Fine Line,
who stand between the poem and nothing?

The ultimate self-effacement is not
the pretense of the minimal,
but the jocular considerations of the maximal
in the manner of Wallace Stevens.

Now it is time, Fine Line, to use the language
that handles everything and is itself
in the same way that it is not itself.

A man who does not wish to be identified
said that no one he knows is happy.

What the deceased knew about birds
flew mistily out of his head when he died.

There is no romance in anticipation
just as there is no steel in bridges.

The days are ahead
1,926,346 to 1,926,345.
Later the nights will catch up.

A man sitting in a cafeteria
had one enormous ear
and one tiny one.
Which was fake?

When X. was 37 he celebrated his 49th and 50th
birthdays to get them out of the way.

It rained in London on April 9th, 1761.
On April 9th, 1934
Nancy Stetson was born.

D. recommends sleep.
He sleeps and is happy.
He thinks I should sleep more.

Many bad poets are incredibly ugly.
Some good ones are, too.

Some beautiful poets are very good.
Some bad ones are, too.

When X. was alone he said,
All of this is unreal.

Take my side
and there will be nothing left of me.

First I considered her in the pale setting of circumstance,
then beyond it, in the whiteness of no one's making.

The generals of desire are often followed by
the barking dogmas of the heart.

Patience is the spectre of want.

My abstention only feeds my enemies.

Poets have so little to gain,
so little to lose,
that they can afford to be jealous.

The self is an allegory
and the Good Knight
is the kiss of the mother
who is the father
who is the mother.

White flags of my breath
when will you surrender?

November 3rd: Today is no exception.

The first line for a play:
Are you taking your cats to Mexico?

Overheard at a dinner party:
Did you never see that crow again?

If she were real I wouldn't let her into this apartment.

If I concentrate for a moment,
I can remember the stillness
of the previous moment.

November 5th: Tomorrow yes.

Headline:
MEXICO'S TREE OF SAD NIGHT SLOWLY DYING

Okay, Wings, do your work.

Waste makes haste
or
I must run from the dump.

Several days later . . .
A few weeks, maybe.
No mail.
Snow.
No desire to continue.
One of my dogs was eaten by the other dogs.

DARKER

I   *Giving Myself Up*

THE NEW POETRY HANDBOOK

for Greg Orr and Greg Simon

1 If a man understands a poem,
    he shall have troubles.

2 If a man lives with a poem,
    he shall die lonely.

3 If a man lives with two poems,
    he shall be unfaithful to one.

4 If a man conceives of a poem,
    he shall have one less child.

5 If a man conceives of two poems,
    he shall have two children less.

6 If a man wears a crown on his head as he writes,
    he shall be found out.

7 If a man wears no crown on his head as he writes,
    he shall deceive no one but himself.

8 If a man gets angry at a poem,
    he shall be scorned by men.

9 If a man continues to be angry at a poem,
    he shall be scorned by women.

10 If a man publicly denounces poetry,
    his shoes will fill with urine.

11 If a man gives up poetry for power,
    he shall have lots of power.

12 If a man brags about his poems,
    he shall be loved by fools.

13 If a man brags about his poems and loves fools,
    he shall write no more.

14   If a man denies his poems pleasure,
       his wit shall wear boots.

15   If a man craves attention because of his poems,
       he shall be like a jackass in moonlight.

16   If a man writes a poem and praises the poem of a
                         fellow,
       he shall have a beautiful mistress.

17   If a man writes a poem and praises the poem of a
                       fellow overly,
       he shall drive his mistress away.

18   If a man claims the poem of another,
       his heart shall double in size.

19   If a man lets his poems go naked,
       he shall fear death.

20   If a man fears death,
       he shall be saved by his poems.

21   If a man does not fear death,
       he may or may not be saved by his poems.

22   If a man finishes a poem,
       he shall bathe in the blank wake of his passion
       and be kissed by white paper.

BREATH

When you see them
tell them I am still here,
that I stand on one leg while the other one dreams,
that this is the only way,

that the lies I tell them are different
from the lies I tell myself,
that by being both here and beyond
I am becoming a horizon,

that as the sun rises and sets I know my place,
that breath is what saves me,
that even the forced syllables of decline are breath,
that if the body is a coffin it is also a closet of breath,

that breath is a mirror clouded by words,
that breath is all that survives the cry for help
as it enters the stranger's ear
and stays long after the word is gone,

that breath is the beginning again, that from it
all resistance falls away, as meaning falls
away from life, or darkness falls from light,
that breath is what I give them when I send my love.

LETTER

for Richard Howard

Men are running across a field,
pens fall from their pockets.
People out walking will pick them up.
It is one of the ways letters are written.

How things fall to others!
The self no longer belonging to me, but asleep
in a stranger's shadow, now clothing
the stranger, now leading him off.

It is noon as I write to you.
Someone's life has come into my hands.
The sun whitens the buildings.
It is all I have. I give it all to you. Yours,

GIVING MYSELF UP

I give up my eyes which are glass eggs.

I give up my tongue.

I give up my mouth which is the constant dream of my
 tongue.

I give up my throat which is the sleeve of my voice.

I give up my heart which is a burning apple.

I give up my lungs which are trees that have never seen
 the moon.

I give up my smell which is that of a stone traveling
 through rain.

I give up my hands which are ten wishes.

I give up my arms which have wanted to leave me anyway.

I give up my legs which are lovers only at night.

I give up my buttocks which are the moons of childhood.

I give up my penis which whispers encouragement to my
 thighs.

I give up my clothes which are walls that blow in the wind
and I give up the ghost that lives in them.

I give up. I give up.

And you will have none of it because already I am beginning
again without anything.

TOMORROW

Your best friend is gone,
your other friend, too.
Now the dream that used to turn in your sleep,
like a diamond, sails into the year's coldest night.

What did you say?
Or was it something you did?
It makes no difference—the house of breath collapsing
around your voice, your voice burning, are nothing to worry
        about.

Tomorrow your friends will cone back;
your moist open mouth will bloom in the glass of storefronts.
Yes. Yes. Tomorrow they will come back and you
will invent an ending that comes out right.

THE ROOM

It is an old story, the way it happens
sometimes in winter, sometimes not.
The listener falls to sleep,
the doors to the closets of his unhappiness open

and into his room the misfortunes come—
death by daybreak, death by nightfall,
their wooden wings bruising the air,
their shadows the spilled milk the world cries over.

There is a need for surprise endings;
the green field where cows burn like newsprint,
where the farmer sits and stares,
where nothing, when it happens, is never terrible enough.

NOSTALGIA

for Donald Justice

The professors of English have taken their gowns
to the laundry, have taken themselves to the fields.
Dreams of motion circle the Persian rug in a room you
        were in.
On the beach the sadness of gramophones
deepens the ocean's folding and falling.
It is yesterday. It is still yesterday.

THE REMAINS

for Bill and Sandy Bailey

I empty myself of the names of others. I empty my pockets.
I empty my shoes and leave them beside the road.
At night I turn back the clocks;
I open the family album and look at myself as a boy.

What good does it do? The hours have done their job.
I say my own name. I say goodbye.
The words follow each other downwind.
I love my wife but send her away.

My parents rise out of their thrones
into the milky rooms of clouds. How can I sing?
Time tells me what I am. I change and I am the same.
I empty myself of my life and my life remains.

THE DANCE

The ghost of another comes to visit and we hold
communion while the light shines.
While the light shines, what else can we do?
And who doesn't have one foot in the grave?

I notice how the trees seem shaggy with leaves
and the steam of insects engulfs them.
The light falls like an anchor through the branches.
And which one of us is not being pulled down constantly?

My mind floats in the purple air of my skull.
I see myself dancing. I smile at everybody.
Slowly I dance out of the burning house of my head.
And who isn't borne again and again into heaven?

THE GOOD LIFE

You stand at the window.
There is a glass cloud in the shape of a heart.
There are the wind's sighs that are like caves in your speech.
You are the ghost in the tree outside.

The street is quiet.
The weather, like tomorrow, like your life,
is partially here, partially up in the air.
There is nothing you can do.

The good life gives no warning.
It weathers the climates of despair
and appears, on foot, unrecognized, offering nothing,
and you are there.

THE DRESS

Lie down on the bright hill
with the moon's hand on your cheek,
your flesh deep in the white folds of your dress,
and you will not hear the passionate mole
extending the length of his darkness,
or the owl arranging all of the night,
which is his wisdom, or the poem
filling your pillow with its blue feathers.
But if you step out of your dress and move into the shade,
the mole will find you, so will the owl, and so will the poem,
and you will fall into another darkness, one you will find
yourself making and remaking until it is perfect.

THE GUARDIAN

The sun setting. The lawns on fire.
The lost day, the lost light.
Why do I love what fades?

You who left, who were leaving,
what dark rooms do you inhabit?
Guardian of my death,

preserve my absence. I am alive.

THE HILL

I have come this far on my own legs,
missing the bus, missing taxis,
climbing always. One foot in front of the other,
that is the way I do it.

It does not bother me, the way the hill goes on.
Grass beside the road, a tree rattling
its black leaves. So what?
The longer I walk, the farther I am from everything.

One foot in front of the other. The hours pass.
One foot in front of the other. The years pass.
The colors of arrival fade.
That is the way I do it.

COMING TO THIS

We have done what we wanted.
We have discarded dreams, preferring the heavy industry
of each other, and we have welcomed grief
and called ruin the impossible habit to break.

And now we are here.
The dinner is ready and we cannot eat.
The meat sits in the white lake of its dish.
The wine waits.

Coming to this
has its rewards: nothing is promised, nothing is taken away.
We have no heart or saving grace,
no place to go, no reason to remain.

II   *Black Maps*

THE SLEEP

There is the sleep of my tongue
speaking a language I can never remember—
words that enter the sleep of words
once they are spoken.

There is the sleep of one moment
inside the next, lengthening the night,
and the sleep of the window
turning the tall sleep of trees into glass.

The sleep of novels as they are read is soundless
like the sleep of dresses on the warm bodies of women.
And the sleep of thunder gathering dust on sunny days
and the sleep of ashes long after.

The sleep of wind has been known to fill the sky.
The long sleep of air locked in the lungs of the dead.
The sleep of a room with someone inside it.
Even the wooden sleep of the moon is possible.

And there is the sleep that demands I lie down
and be fitted to the dark that comes upon me
like another skin in which I shall never be found,
out of which I shall never appear.

BLACK MAPS

Not the attendance of stones,
nor the applauding wind,
shall let you know
you have arrived,

nor the sea that celebrates
only departures,
nor the mountains,
nor the dying cities.

Nothing will tell you
where you are.
Each moment is a place
you've never been.

You can walk
believing you cast
a light around you.
But how will you know?

The present is always dark.
Its maps are black,
rising from nothing,
describing,

in their slow ascent
into themselves,
their own voyage,
its emptiness,

the bleak, temperate
necessity of its completion.
As they rise into being
they are like breath.

And if they are studied at all
it is only to find,
too late, what you thought
were concerns of yours

do not exist.
Your house is not marked
on any of them,
nor are your friends,

waiting for you to appear,
nor are your enemies,
listing your faults.
Only you are there,

saying hello
to what you will be,
and the black grass
is holding up the black stars.

SEVEN POEMS

for Antonia

1

At the edge
of the body's night
ten moons are rising.

2

A scar remembers the wound.
The wound remembers the pain.
Once more you are crying.

3

When we walk in the sun
our shadows are like barges of silence.

4

My body lies down
and I hear my own
voice lying next to me.

5

The rock is pleasure
and it opens
and we enter it
as we enter ourselves
each night.

6

When I talk to the window
I say everything
is everything.

7

I have a key
so I open the door and walk in.
It is dark and I walk in.
It is darker and I walk in.

FROM A LITANY

There in an open field I lie down in a hole I once dug and I
praise the sky.

I praise the clouds that are like lungs of light.

I praise the owl that wants to inhabit me and the hawk that
does not.

I praise the mouse's fury, the wolf's consideration.

I praise the dog that lives in the household of people and shall
never be one of them.

I praise the whale that lives under the cold blankets of salt.

I praise the formations of squid, the domes of meandra.

I praise the secrecy of doors, the openness of windows.

I praise the depth of closets.

I praise the wind, the rising generations of air.

I praise the trees on whose branches shall sit the Cock of
Portugal and the Polish Cock.

I praise the palm trees of Rio and those that shall grow in
London.

I praise the gardeners, the worms and the small plants that
praise each other.

I praise the sweet berries of Georgetown, Maine and the song
of the white-throated sparrow.

I praise the poets of Waverly Place and Eleventh Street, and
the one whose bones turn to dark emeralds when he
stands upright in the wind.

I praise the clocks for which I grow old in a day and young in
a day.

I praise all manner of shade, that which I see and that which
I do not.

I praise all roofs from the watery roof of the pond to the slate
 roof of the customs house.
I praise those who have made of their bodies final embassies of
 flesh.
I praise the failure of those with ambition, the authors of
 leaflets and notebooks of nothing.
I praise the moon for suffering men.
I praise the sun its tributes.
I praise the pain of revival and the bliss of decline.
I praise all for nothing because there is no price.
I praise myself for the way I have with a shovel and I praise
 the shovel.
I praise the motive of praise by which I shall be reborn.
I praise the morning whose sun is upon me.
I praise the evening whose son I am.

THE RECOVERY

I stood alone in the weather
and wished I were wrapped in the stones,
the long sheets, the bones of my father
laid out in the ground, and later,

after waiting, and watching
the sun fall into the hills and the night
close down over the least light,
I walked to the water's edge

and saw the doctors wave from the deck of a boat
that steamed from port, their bags open,
their instruments shining like ruins under the moon,
and it was no more than anyone might have predicted.

THE PREDICTION

That night the moon drifted over the pond,
turning the water to milk, and under
the boughs of the trees, the blue trees,
a young woman walked, and for an instant

the future came to her:
rain falling on her husband's grave, rain falling
on the lawns of her children, her own mouth
filling with cold air, strangers moving into her house,

a man in her room writing a poem, the moon drifting
        into it,
a woman strolling under its trees, thinking of death,
thinking of him thinking of her, and the wind rising
and taking the moon and leaving the paper dark.

THE ONE SONG

I prefer to sit all day
like a sack in a chair
and to lie all night
like a stone in my bed.

When food comes
I open my mouth.
When sleep comes
I close my eyes.

My body sings
only one song;
the wind turns
gray in my arms.

Flowers bloom.
Flowers die.
More is less.
I long for more.

THE STONE

The stone lives on.
The followers of the man with the glass face
walk around it
with their glass legs
and glass arms.

The stone lives on.
It lives on air.
It lives on your looking.
It lives inside and outside
itself and is never clear
which is which.

That is why
the followers of the man with the glass face
walk around it proposing
the possibilities
of emptiness.

The stone lives on,
commending itself to the hardness of air,
to the long meadows of your looking.

FROM A LITANY

Let the shark keep to the shelves and closets of coral.
Let cats throw over their wisdom.
Let the noble horse who rocks under the outlaw's ass eat
        plastic turf.
For no creature is safe.
Let the great sow of state grow strong.
Let those in office search under their clothes for the private
        life.
They will find nothing.
Let them gather together and hold hands.
They shall have nothing to hold.
Let the flag flutter in the glass moon of each eye.
Let the black-suited priests stand for the good life.
Let them tell us to be more like them.
For that is the nature of the sickness.
Let the bodies of debutantes gleam like frigidaires.
For they shall have sex with food.
Let flies sink into their mothers' thighs and go blind in
        the trenches of meat.
Let the patient unmask the doctor and swim in the gray
        milk of his mind.
For nothing will keep.
Let the bleak faces of the police swell like yeast.
Let breezes run like sauce over their skins.
For this kingdom is theirs.
Let a violet cloak fall on the bleached hair of the poetess.

Let twilight cover the lost bone of her passion.
For her moon is ambition.
Let the dusty air release its sugars.
Let candy the color of marlin flesh build up on the tables.
For everyone's mouth is open.
Let the wind devise secrets and leave them in trees.
Let the earth suck at roots and discover the emblems of
     weather.

III *My Life By Somebody Else*

MY LIFE

The huge doll of my body
refuses to rise.
I am the toy of women.
My mother

would prop me up for her friends.
"Talk, talk," she would beg.
I moved my mouth
but words did not come.

My wife took me down from the shelf.
I lay in her arms. "We suffer
the sickness of self," she would whisper.
And I lay there dumb.

Now my daughter
gives me a plastic nurser
filled with water.
"You are my real baby," she says.

Poor child!
I look into the brown
mirrors of her eyes
and see myself

diminishing, sinking down
to a depth she does not know is there.
Out of breath,
I will not rise again.

I grow into my death.
My life is small
and getting smaller. The world is green.
Nothing is all.

MY DEATH

Sadness, of course, and confusion.
The relatives gathered at the graveside,
talking about the waste, and the weather mounting,
the rain moving in vague pillars offshore.

This is Prince Edward Island.
I came back to my birthplace to announce my death.
I said I would ride full gallop into the sea
and not look back. People were furious.

I told them about attempts I had made in the past,
how I starved in order to be the size of Lucille,
whom I loved, to inhabit the cold space
her body had taken. They were shocked.

I went on about the time
I dove in a perfect arc that filled
with the sunshine of farewell and I fell
head over shoulders into the river's thigh.

And about the time
I stood naked in the snow, pointing a pistol
between my eyes, and how when I fired my head bloomed
into health. Soon I was alone.

Now I lie in the box
of my making while the weather
builds and the mourners shake their heads as if
to write or to die, I did not have to do either.

MY LIFE BY SOMEBODY ELSE

I have done what I could but you avoid me.
I left a bowl of milk on the desk to tempt you.
Nothing happened. I left my wallet there, full of money.
You must have hated me for that. You never came.

I sat at my typewriter naked, hoping you would wrestle me
to the floor. I played with myself just to arouse you.
Boredom drove me to sleep. I offered you my wife.
I sat her on the desk and spread her legs. I waited.

The days drag on. The exhausted light falls like a
        bandage
over my eyes. Is it because I am ugly? Was anyone
ever so sad? It is pointless to slash my wrists. My hands
would fall off. And then what hope would I have?

Why do you never come? Must I have you by being
somebody else? Must I write *My Life* by somebody else?
My Death by somebody else? Are you listening?
Somebody else has arrived. Somebody else is writing.

COURTSHIP

There is a girl you like so you tell her
your penis is big, but that you cannot get yourself
to use it. Its demands are ridiculous, you say,
even self-defeating, but to be honored somehow,
briefly, inconspicuously in the dark.

When she closes her eyes in horror,
you take it all back. You tell her you're almost
a girl yourself and can understand why she is shocked.
When she is about to walk away, you tell her
you have no penis, that you don't

know what got into you. You get on your knees.
She suddenly bends down to kiss your shoulder and
          you know
you're on the right track. You tell her you want
to bear children and that is why you seem confused.
You wrinkle your brow and curse the day you were born.

She tries to calm you, but you lose control.
You reach for her panties and beg forgiveness as you do.
She squirms and you howl like a wolf. Your craving
seems monumental. You know you will have her.
Taken by storm, she is the girl you will marry.

ELEGY 1969

You slave away into your old age
and nothing you do adds up to much.
Day after day you go through the same motions,
you shiver in bed, you get hungry, you want a woman.

Heroes standing for lives of sacrifice and obedience
fill the parks through which you walk.
At night in the fog they open their bronze umbrellas
or else withdraw to the empty lobbies of movie houses.

You love the night for its power of annihilating,
but while you sleep, your problems will not let you die.
Waking only proves the existence of The Great Machine
and the hard light falls on your shoulders.

You walk among the dead and talk
about times to come and matters of the spirit.
Literature wasted your best hours of love-making.
Weekends were lost, cleaning your apartment.

You are quick to confess your failure and to postpone
collective joy to the next century. You accept
rain, war, unemployment and the unjust distribution of
      wealth
because you can't, all by yourself, blow up Manhattan
      Island.

(AFTER CARLOS DRUMMOND DE ANDRADE)

"THE DREADFUL HAS ALREADY HAPPENED"

The relatives are leaning over, staring expectantly.
They moisten their lips with their tongues. I can feel
them urging me on. I hold the baby in the air.
Heaps of broken bottles glitter in the sun.

A small band is playing old fashioned marches.
My mother is keeping time by stamping her foot.
My father is kissing a woman who keeps waving
to somebody else. There are palm trees.

The hills are spotted with orange flamboyants and tall
billowy clouds move behind them. "Go on, Boy,"
I hear somebody say, "Go on."
I keep wondering if it will rain.

The sky darkens. There is thunder.
"Break his legs," says one of my aunts,
"Now give him a kiss." I do what I'm told.
The trees bend in the bleak tropical wind.

The baby did not scream, but I remember that sigh
when I reached inside for his tiny lungs and shook them
out in the air for the flies. The relatives cheered.
It was about that time I gave up.

Now, when I answer the phone, his lips
are in the receiver; when I sleep, his hair is gathered
around a familiar face on the pillow; wherever I search
I find his feet. He is what is left of my life.

NOT DYING

These wrinkles are nothing.
These gray hairs are nothing.
This stomach which sags
with old food, these bruised
and swollen ankles,
my darkening brain,
they are nothing.
I am the same boy
my mother used to kiss.

The years change nothing.
On windless summer nights
I feel those kisses
slide from her dark
lips far away,
and in winter they float
over the frozen pines
and arrive covered with snow.
They keep me young.

My passion for milk
is uncontrollable still.
I am driven by innocence.
From bed to chair I crawl
and back again.
I shall not die.
The grave result
and token of birth, my body
remembers and holds fast.

THE WAY IT IS

The world is ugly
And the people are sad.
WALLACE STEVENS

I lie in bed.
I toss all night
in the cold unruffled deep
of my sheets and cannot sleep.

My neighbor marches in his room,
wearing the sleek
mask of a hawk with a large beak.
He stands by the window. A violet plume

rises from his helmet's dome.
The moon's light
spills over him like milk and the wind rinses the white
glass bowls of his eyes.

His helmet in a shopping bag,
he sits in the park, waving a small American flag.
He cannot be heard as he moves
behind trees and hedges,

always at the frayed edges
of town, pulling a gun on someone like me. I crouch
under the kitchen table, telling myself
I am a dog, who would kill a dog?

My neighbor's wife comes home.
She walks into the living room,
takes off her clothes, her hair falls down her back.
She seems to wade

through long flat rivers of shade.
The soles of her feet are black.
She kisses her husband's neck
and puts her hands inside his pants.

My neighbors dance.
They roll on the floor, his tongue
is in her ear, his lungs
reek with the swill and weather of hell.

Out on the street people are lying down
with their knees in the air, tears
fill their eyes, ashes
enter their ears.

Their clothes are torn
from their backs. Their faces are worn.
Horsemen are riding around them, telling them why
they should die.

My neighbor's wife calls to me, her mouth is pressed
against the wall behind my bed.
She says, "My husband's dead."
I turn over on my side,

hoping she has not lied.
The walls and ceiling of my room are gray—
the moon's color through the windows of a laundromat.
I close my eyes.

I see myself float
on the dead sea of my bed, falling away.
calling for help, but the vague scream
sticks in my throat.

I see myself in the park
on horseback, surrounded by dark,
leading the armies of peace.
The iron legs of the horse do not bend.

I drop the reins. Where will the turmoil end?
Fleets of taxis stall
in the fog, passengers fall
asleep. Gas pours

from a tri-colored stack.
Locking their doors,
people from offices huddle together,
telling the same story over and over.

Everyone who has sold himself wants to buy himself back.
Nothing is done. The night
eats into their limbs
like a blight.

Everything dims.
The future is not what it used to be.
The graves are ready. The dead
shall inherit the dead.

A NOTE ABOUT THE AUTHOR

Mark Strand was born in Summerside, Prince Edward Island, Canada, and was raised and educated in the United States and South America. He is the author of eight books of poems, the most recent of which was *The Continuous Life*, published in 1990. His book of short stories *Mr. and Mrs. Baby* was published in 1985. His translations include *The Owl's Insomnia*, a selection of Rafael Alberti's poems, and *Travelling in the Family*, a selection of Carlos Drummond de Andrade's poems, edited in collaboration with Thomas Colchie. He has written several children's books, and edited several anthologies, including *Another Republic*, which he coedited with Charles Simic. He has published numerous articles and essays on painting and photography, and in 1987 his book on William Bailey was published. He has been the recipient of fellowships from the Ingram Merrill, Rockefeller and Guggenheim Foundations and from the National Endowment for the Arts. In 1979 he was awarded the Fellowship of the Academy of American Poets, and in 1987 he received a John D. and Catherine T. MacArthur Fellowship. He has taught at many colleges and universities, and since 1981 has been a professor of English at the University of Utah. In 1990 he was chosen by the Librarian of Congress to be Poet Laureate of the United States. He lives in Salt Lake City with his wife and son.

A NOTE ON THE TYPE

This book is set in Monotype BASKERVILLE, a facsimile cutting from type cast from the original matrices of a face designed by John Baskerville. The original face was the forerunner of the "modern" group of type faces. John Baskerville (1706–75), of Birmingham, England, a writing-master, with a special renown for cutting inscriptions in stone, began experimenting about 1750 with punch-cutting and making typographical material. It was not until 1757 that he published his first work, a Virgil in royal quarto, with great-primer letters. This was followed by his famous editions of Milton, the Bible, the Book of Common Prayer, and several Latin classic authors. His types, at first criticized as unnecessarily slender, delicate, and feminine, in time were recognized as both distinct and elegant, and his types as well as his printing were greatly admired. Four years after his death Baskerville's widow sold all his punches and matrices to the Société Littéraire-typographique, which used some of the types for the sumptuous Kehl edition of Voltaire's works in seventy volumes.

Composition by Heritage Printers, Inc.,
Charlotte, North Carolina
Printed and bound by Halliday Lithographers,
West Hanover, Massachusetts